Witch*Wendy

Books by Alex Gutteridge

Witch Wendy

1. Cats and Hats
2. Broom Broom!
3. Cat Tricks

Witch✷Wendy

Cat
Tricks

Alex Gutteridge

Illustrated by Annabel Hudson

MACMILLAN CHILDREN'S BOOKS

For Brenda

First published 2002 by Macmillan Children's Books Ltd
a division of Macmillan Publishers Limited
20 New Wharf Road, London N1 9RR
Basingstoke and Oxford
www.panmacmillan.com

Associated companies throughout the world

ISBN 0 330 39852 0

1 3 5 7 9 8 6 4 2

A CIP catalogue record for this book is available from
the British Library.

Typeset by Macmillan Publishers Limited
Printed and bound in Great Britain by Mackays of Chatham plc, Kent

Chapter One

Witch Wendy was in a flap. She was late for the weekly witches' meeting again and her broomstick refused to go any faster.

"Witch Rosemary is so cross if we're not on time," Wendy moaned. "She's bound to cast a spiteful spell on me."

Snowflake, her cat, clung to the back of the broomstick. He was all of a quiver.

"Coalface is so catty when we're late," he groaned. "He's bound to sharpen his claws on me."

The broomstick crashed into the kerb and screeched to a stop outside

the Hairy Wart pub. There was a dreadful din coming from inside. It was the sound of whooping wizards and wittering witches.

Wendy gave Snowflake a little pat. Snowflake rubbed his cheek along the side of Wendy's shoe. They sidled into the Cock's Tail Bar together.

"We're not too late, are we?" Wendy whispered to Snowflake. "Rosemary won't be too mean . . . will she?"

"She looks in a t-terrible t-temper to me," Snowflake stuttered. "And Coalface looks like a real sour puss."

Snowflake pointed to the dingiest, darkest corner where a horrible

hunched-up figure squatted on a stool. On her lap was a furious-faced cat. Wendy trembled from the point of her hat down to the tips of her toenails.

"Oh dear," she said. "Wait for the snarling."

"And the spitting," Snowflake frowned.

"And the scratching," Wendy quaked.

"And that's just Rosemary," Snowflake sighed.

Wendy jumped as someone yanked

at her hair. "Ouch!" she shrieked, spinning around.

Witch Harriet and Witch Primrose stood behind her.

"Here you are at last," tut-tutted Primrose.

"Rosemary wouldn't wait," Harriet sniffed. "We had the Magic Meeting without you."

"Did I miss anything important?" Wendy murmured.

Primrose and Harriet looked at each other. They gulped. They sniggered. Then they jutted out their hairy chins and laughed and laughed.

"What's the matter with *them*?" Wendy asked Snowflake.

"More importantly," Snowflake whispered, "what's the matter with Rosemary?"

Witch Rosemary sat silently in the corner.

"No roaring with rage," Wendy said.

"No hateful hissing," Snowflake added, feeling anxious.

"In fact," Wendy murmured, "it's . . . "

". . . scary," they both said together.

Wendy decided to be brave. She straightened her traffic cone hat, stretched her short body as tall as it would go and walked up to the warty old witch.

"Are you all right, Rosemary?" Wendy asked.

Rosemary twitched and lifted her head. She pulled a horrible face, stuck out a furry tongue and gave a faint gurgle.

Wendy peered at her. Her skin was grisly green and her eyes glowed sickly yellow as usual, but she didn't seem herself. Primrose and Harriet both looked sad.

"Poor Rosemary," Primrose sniffled.

"It's the most terrible news," Harriet gulped.

"She's lost her cackle," Primrose cried. "It wafted away on the West wind and didn't come back."

Snowflake started to smile. Wendy tried hard not to laugh.

"So," Wendy said, "Rosemary can't talk?"

Primrose and Harriet shook their heads and each shed three tears.

"It's a tragedy," Harriet wailed. "Rosemary is completely and utterly screechless!"

Chapter Two

"Are you still a scaredy cat?" Wendy asked Snowflake.

He shook his head.

"Are you still a twitchy witch?" Snowflake asked Wendy.

She shook her head.

"There won't be any mean magic

from Rosemary tonight," Snowflake sniggered. "We can relax."

Harriet's cat, Sable, was curled up in front of the fire. Snowflake strolled up to her. "That colour fur really suits you, Sable," he gushed. "You should wear it more often."

"I think I'm going to be sick," said Primrose's cat, Nightshade.

Snowflake ignored him. Sable smiled. Snowflake felt his legs wobble.

"You seem very cheerful," she purred, "considering."

Snowflake stared into her beautiful blue eyes. "Considering what?" he asked dreamily.

"You obviously haven't heard the news," Nightshade smirked.

"Rosemary has to go into hospital, so Coalface is coming to stay."

Snowflake admired the way Sable's whiskers fanned out neatly.

"Poor you," murmured Snowflake.

"You just don't understand, do you?" Sable sang in her velvety voice. "The witches took a vote before you arrived. Coalface is coming to stay with *you*!"

As soon as they got home Snowflake went straight to bed.

"My life is ruined," he moaned, "for ever and ever!"

"Nonsense," Wendy said. "It's only for a few nights while Rosemary goes to the Cackle Clinic to get a new screech. Perhaps Coalface isn't so bad once you get to know him properly."

"Perhaps dogs don't bark and the night isn't dark," Snowflake sobbed.

"Of course he's bad! He fights and he bites and he's always making catty comments!"

"Well, we've just got to make the best of it," said Wendy. "Now try and get some rest. He'll be here first thing in the evening."

"I shall have daymares," Snowflake snuffled. "I won't sleep properly. I shall have to take cat naps when he's not around."

"Snowflake," Wendy said, snuggling down in her bed. "It's for three nights. How bad can it be?"

"It won't just be bad," muttered Snowflake. "It'll be the pits."

Chapter Three

Snowflake woke up with a start. An amber eye glinted at the keyhole and heavy breathing slithered through the letter box.

"Oi, fishbreath," someone grunted. "Let me in."

"You're too early," said Snowflake.

"It's barely dark."

"I'm cold and I'm wet and I'm very hungry," Coalface grunted. "Now let me in or I'll caterwaul loudly enough to wake all the witches in the world."

Snowflake opened the door and Coalface strolled in. He glanced around the room. Wendy was still snoring soundly in her bed.

"This isn't like a witch's house at all." Coalface wrinkled up his nose. "It's clean and tidy, and it smells disgusting."

"That's Herbfresh furniture polish," Snowflake said.

"But where are the spiders and the piles of mouse droppings? Where is the cauldron full of gunge and the slime running down the walls? Where is the *mess*?" Coalface growled.

Wendy woke up and jumped out of bed. "Coalface! How . . . lovely to see you. Has Snowflake got you any breakfast?"

"Fish is my favourite," Coalface smirked.

"Since when?" Snowflake whispered.

"Since a second ago," he chuckled, sharpening his claws on the table leg.

Snowflake buried his face in his paws as Wendy opened the cupboard and took out his special tin of pilchards. She gave it all to Coalface. Then she went into the kitchen and came back with his best bowl, full of cream. She gave that to Coalface too.

Snowflake scowled and gave a tiny growl.

"We must make him feel welcome," Wendy whispered, "or he might turn nasty."

"Yummy," murmured Coalface as he

crunched the
pilchards. Then
he spat the
bones out on
to the carpet.

"Scrummy," gurgled Coalface as he lapped up the cream. Then he wiped his mouth on the tablecloth and burped. "Perhaps it's not so bad here after all," he scowled.

Coalface padded over to Snowflake's basket. He got in it. Snowflake stared at Wendy. He glared at Wendy. She gave him a sorry smile. Coalface yawned loudly.

"It's been so quiet since Rosemary

lost her cackle," he said. "I'm quite worn out!" He closed his eyes and went to sleep.

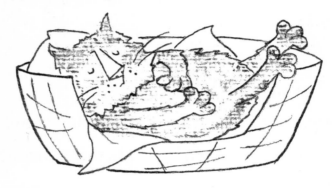

"Well," said Wendy happily, "he seems to have made himself at home."

She picked up her wand from the table and skipped across the room. She paused in front of a pale-pink door with a silver handle in the shape of a star.

"While Coalface is resting,
I'll make some potions
in my Pink Pantry."

"Can you find
something to make
him disappear?"
Snowflake called, but Wendy had
already slipped through the door and
closed it firmly behind her.

Snowflake swept up the fish bones,
put the tablecloth in the washing
machine and fitted a big
padlock to the fish cupboard.

Snowflake
heard a tap at
the window. He

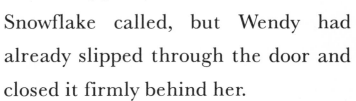

looked up. Nightshade and Sable pressed their noses to the glass.

"Has he arrived?" Sable asked.

"Has he been bad?" asked Nightshade.

"He's eaten all my prize pilchards, finished off the cream, and he's sleeping in my basket," replied Snowflake. "And he's got disgusting table manners."

"Oh dear," murmured Sable. "You're such a hero to put up with him."

"Do you think so?" Snowflake perked up. He smiled his most charming smile. "Well, if Coalface gets too troublesome I'll just get rid of him."

"You wouldn't dare!" Sable cried.

"I would," bluffed Snowflake. "I'm not the cowardly cat you seem to think I am."

"Hmph," said Nightshade. "I think you're all growls and no bite. But don't send him to us if you do throw him out."

"But he hasn't done anything really terrible, has he?" Sable asked.

"No," Snowflake replied and a shiver ran up his spine, "not yet."

Chapter Four

"I've just got to nip out," Wendy said the next night. "It's against the Flyway Code to take two cats on a broomstick so you'll have to stay here."

"Don't worry," Coalface smiled. "I'll make sure Snowball behaves himself."

Snowflake winced. He knew for sure there was trouble ahead.

As soon as Wendy had gone Coalface stretched, flexed his claws and padded towards Snowflake.

"Let's have some fun," he smirked.

"Do . . . do we have to?" Snowflake stammered.

Coalface leaned against the door to Wendy's pantry.

"You can't go in there," said Snowflake.

"Why not?" Coalface rattled the door handle.

"Cats aren't allowed in witches' pantries on their own."

"I can go anywhere I like," said Coalface with a gruesome grin.

He pushed the door open. "It's not even locked," he purred. "Wendy must be a witless witch to be so trusting."

Along the walls of the Pink Pantry were dozens of pearly pink bottles. Each one had a pretty label stuck to the front of it.

"This isn't a proper witch's pantry," Coalface sneered. "Look at all these things: hugging humbugs, caring crystals, rosy raindrops. Pah! Where are the ponging pills and the dreadful dandruff and the beetle blood?"

"We've got mouth-watering mice," Snowflake bristled, "or—"

"*Witch Wendy's Simple Spells*," Coalface chuckled, picking up a battered book from the table.

"You can't touch that," said Snowflake as Coalface opened the book.

"I can't read what it says." Coalface squinted at the words. "She's got terrible handwriting. Does this say mouse or house?"

"I don't do spells," Snowflake said. He started to feel sick.

"Witch Rosemary often trusts me to do her spells," Coalface boasted. "There is a certain way to do it, of course, and you have to be a special sort of cat. Stylish, handsome, CLEVER."

He looked down his scabby nose at Snowflake. "Perhaps that's why you've never been allowed to make magic. I'll show you how it's done."

"You needn't bother," Snowflake said.

"I'm not leaving this room until I've stirred up a spell," Coalface growled, leafing through the book. "What about Pong of Skunks?"

Snowflake wrinkled up his nose and peeked over Coalface's shoulder.

"Are you sure that doesn't say Song of Monks?"

Coalface hissed and turned the page. "Well, what about Glowering Gloom? That sounds fun."

"Mmm," said Snowflake, "except it could say Flowers in Bloom."

"Yuk!" Coalface grizzled.

"What about this small spell," Snowflake said, "for a blue bottle?"

"Boring!" Coalface yawned.

"But at least we can read it. And Wendy will be back soon."

"All right, Snowy," Coalface snapped.

"Get me a wand."

He took a pink bottle off the shelf and put it on the table.

Snowflake grabbed the nearest wand. It had a label attached to it.

"A Willing Wand," Coalface read, sneering. "How sweet."

"Oh!" Snowflake said. "Are you sure the label says willing?"

"Purrfectly sure." Coalface grinned.

He whisked the wand through the air. He jerked it forwards, he jolted it backwards. Sparks sprinkled out of

the wand and smoke swirled around
the room. He pointed the wand at the
pretty pink bottle.

"With a waving wand at full throttle,
Be transformed into a bluebottle!"

As Coalface chanted the last two
words of the spell, the wand wobbled
wildly before wilting backwards and

pointing straight at Coalface.

Snowflake shielded his eyes as a blaze of light dazzled the room. Then there was a mournful M-I-A-O-WWWWW, followed by an odd hush.

Snowflake peeped out from behind his paws. The wand lay on the floor and the pink bottle still sat on the table – but Coalface had completely vanished.

Chapter Five

"SNOWFLAKE! What are you doing?" Wendy stood in the doorway. "You know this room is out of bounds."

"I was . . . er . . . chasing some mice," said Snowflake, and he hustled a couple of invisible mice back into their holes.

"Where's Coalface?" Wendy frowned.

"He . . ." Snowflake stammered. "He seems to have disappeared."

"Did he say where he was going?" Wendy asked.

Snowflake shook his head. "He was here one minute and gone the next."

"Snowflake, can I smell a spell?" Wendy's nose twitched.

"Categorically not," Snowflake lied.

Wendy walked over to the table and picked up the wand.

"I hope you haven't been using the Wilting Wand. It

could create all sorts of trouble."

She closed up the *Simple Spell Book*.
A fly flew up from the page and
landed on her hat. She swatted it
away. The fly began to buzz.
Snowflake ducked as a streak of blue
dive-bombed him.

"I've got some good news for you,"
Wendy said. "Rosemary is coming out

of the Cackle Clinic a night early. She'll be here to collect Coalface tomorrow evening."

The fly circled Snowflake's head, giving an extra loud buzz as it went past each ear.

Wendy picked up a fly swatter. She twirled it in her hand and whirled it over her head. She eyed up the fly.

"I can't stand flies," muttered Wendy, "but bluebottles are the worst of all."

"Did you say BLUEBOTTLE?"

Snowflake gasped. He put his head in his paws. "Oh my wilting whiskers!"

"Snowflake," Wendy asked, "what's the matter?"

"Now promise you won't fly into a temper," he replied, "but—"

Suddenly there was a rattling at the windows and a shaking of the walls.

"Coo-ee!" a voice squealed through the letterbox. "We've all come for a midnight feast."

"You'll have to tell me later," Wendy said.

She shooed Snowflake out of the pantry and closed the door behind her with a firm click.

Primrose and Harriet skipped into the sitting room.

"We've brought fabulous fleabread," said Primrose.

"And crunchy caterpillar cake," trilled Harriet.

"I've made jumping jellies and silly sundaes," Wendy giggled. "Let's go and guzzle them in the garden."

"*We've* come for a cat chat." Sable winked at Snowflake once the witches had left the room. "We've brought slivers of liver to keep Coalface happy. It's his favourite."

"Where is Ugly Mug?" asked Nightshade.

"He's . . . um . . . just buzzed off somewhere," said Snowflake.

"That's odd," said Nightshade.

"Especially as he knew that I was coming," Sable pouted.

There was a humming noise coming from behind the Pink Pantry door. Snowflake saw the key wobble in the lock. There was a clunk as it fell to the floor. Six cat's eyes swivelled round. Something shot out through the keyhole and nosedived towards Snowflake.

Snowflake grabbed his flying helmet and ran for cover. The fly tickled his tail, it belly flopped on his back and it needled his nostrils.

"That fly doesn't like you," said Sable.

"It hates you almost as much as Coalface does," said Nightshade.

The two cats exchanged glances. Nightshade threw back his head and yowled.

"It wasn't my fault!" Snowflake protested, batting away the fly.

"When you said you'd get rid of him, I didn't think you meant magic," Nightshade gasped.

"It's incredible," murmured Sable. "Snowflake, you really are the cat's whiskers."

Chapter Six

Snowflake chased Coalface into the Pink Pantry and trapped him under a glass.

"Primrose says reversing spells are so difficult to get right," said Nightshade.

"You *do* know how to turn him

back?" Sable asked.

"Of course," Snowflake fibbed.

"Because if you don't," Nightshade murmured, "you know what the *Witch's Cat Handbook* says?"

"What?" Snowflake asked.

"You'll have to become Witch Rosemary's cat," Sable replied.

Snowflake tried to smile bravely but his teeth chattered together. He tried to laugh but the sound got tangled in his throat and instead it came out as a long, high-pitched howl.

He couldn't think of anything worse than living with Witch Rosemary.

✳

Primrose and Harriet dashed away with their cats just as dawn was breaking.

"Snowflake," Wendy said sternly, "are you sure Coalface didn't say where he was going?"

"Only that he'd got to fly," Snowflake muttered.

"Well, we've got to find him," Wendy said, "or we're both in big trouble."

While Wendy searched the garden, Snowflake padded into the pantry. He scanned the bookshelves.

There were books on *Riotous Recipes* and *Bewitching Buildings*. There were books on *How to Be a Wonderful Witch* and *Fascinating Flyovers of Our Time*, but not one book on undoing spells.

"What am I going to do?" Wendy wailed through the window. "If Rosemary finds out I've lost Coalface she'll banish my broomstick, she'll steal my spell book and . . ."

Wendy gulped.

Her voice dropped to a whisper

". . . and she'll claim my precious cat."

Snowflake went outside and tugged at Wendy's stripy sock with his teeth.

"Come and get some sleep,"

Snowflake said soothingly. "I'll sort everything out."

Snowflake stayed up all day. He searched everywhere for the book to help him undo Coalface's spell. By witches' wake-up time he still hadn't found it.

"I shall have to tell Wendy what's happened," he moaned to himself.

"She probably won't know where the book is, she probably won't be able to get the right spell, and she'll definitely panic. But it's my only hope."

Snowflake took a deep breath and scrambled up on to Wendy's bed. He prodded Wendy gently with his paw. She let out a shuddering snore and turned over. A creased purple pamphlet lay in the space where she had been lying.

Snowflake picked up the slim booklet and read the title: *A Disenchanting Book*.

"I've got it!" Snowflake mewed softly.

He bounded off the bed and rushed into the Pink Pantry. Coalface stared at him from his glass prison. He buzzed as loudly as a mob of bluebottles.

"Be quiet!" Snowflake snapped. "Unless you want me to turn you into a greenfly."

Coalface stopped buzzing, and Snowflake slowly lifted up the glass.

Coalface's big bluebottle eyes bulged angrily, but he stayed quite still.

Snowflake scrabbled through the pages of the purple pamphlet. He picked up a wand with a shaky paw and started the spell.

"Take unbewitching, charmless lore
Make this fly as it was before."

Coalface buzzed briefly but the spell didn't work.

Suddenly the window panes rattled and a horrible noise filled the air. It was a cackle as loud and creepy as any Snowflake had ever heard.

"Oh, my trembling tail," he said. "Witches!"

Coalface buzzed again. He edged backwards across the table.

"Will you stay still?" Snowflake pleaded.

He batted Coalface with his paw. The bluebottle slid into the middle of the table.

Three heavy thuds shook the room and there was a scraping, sliding sound as several tiles slid from the roof and clattered past the window.

They were swiftly followed by three tumbling witches.

"Wendeeeeeeee! It's meeeeeeee!"

Rosemary's voice was as out of tune as ever. Her cackle was crazier and more fur-raising than before.

Snowflake's tail trembled and his legs wobbled. Coalface buzzed backwards, thudding his six bluebottle legs down on the table top.

Snowflake stared at him.

"I wonder," he murmured. "Perhaps if I try the spell backwards."

"Beforewasitasflythismake lorecharmlessunbewitchingtake."

Snowflake couldn't get the words out of his mouth fast enough.

The wand stuttered, it sputtered and Coalface started to spin. As he twizzled he got bigger and bluer and buzzier.

Snowflake closed his eyes.

There was one last huge buzz
followed by a gigantic growl.

Snowflake opened one eye. Standing
in the middle of the table was Coalface
the cat. He looked even bigger and
meaner than before. He wiggled his
furry bottom, he flattened his tattered

ears and he got ready to pounce.

"Now, Coalface." Snowflake smiled weakly. "Don't be too cross. It was you who insisted on showing me how to do a cat spell."

Coalface hissed and edged forwards. Snowflake inched backwards and tried to pull the pantry door open with his back foot.

"You really wouldn't want me to tell everyone that you're not such a clever cat after all, would you?" Snowflake said in a shaky voice.

"Where is he, then?" Rosemary ranted through all the rooms. "Wendy! Where's my moth-eaten moggie?"

Rosemary pushed past Wendy, Primrose and Harriet and marched into the Pink Pantry.

"Rosemary," Wendy ran after her, "I've got something to tell you. I'm so sorry . . . Coalface is missing."

"What?" Rosemary shrieked.

Primrose and Harriet scurried behind a chair and Sable and

Nightshade ran straight up the curtains in fright.

Snowflake spun round and stood on his hind legs in front of Rosemary.

"Missing YOU," he miaowed. "What Wendy means is Coalface is missing YOU."

Snowflake winked slyly at Wendy and secretly blew Sable a kiss as she clung to the curtain pole. There was a scary stillness for a moment.

Rosemary scooped Coalface up and stared into his flashing eyes. He opened his mouth to speak. Snowflake held his breath and wound his tail around Wendy's leg. Then Coalface spat and a shower of saliva hit Snowflake's face.

Rosemary let out an ear-splitting screech.

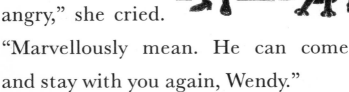

"He's amazingly angry," she cried. "Marvellously mean. He can come and stay with you again, Wendy."

"Snowflake," Wendy said after Rosemary, Primrose and Harriet had left. "Did Coalface say where he had been?"

"I don't think he'd been far," Snowflake murmured as he washed his face for the umpteenth time.

"He was so cross when Rosemary came to fetch him." Wendy mused. "I almost wondered if he was sad to be leaving us. What do you think Snowflake?"

"You could be right," Snowflake licked his paw. "Coalface is probably going to be feeling a bit blue for quite some time!"